Moose Tales

Nancy Van Laan

Illustrated by Amy Rusch

Houghton Mifflin Company
Boston 1999

In memory of my
moose-lovin' buddy, Joyce
—N. V. L.

For Jane Daisy Rusch
March 24, 1914–October 9, 1996
—A. R.

MAR 1 0 2000

Text copyright © 1999 by Nancy Van Laan
Illustrations copyright © 1999 by Amy Rusch

The text of this book is set in 15-point New Century Schoolbook.
The illustrations are ink and colored pencil.

Library of Congress Cataloging-in-Publication Data

Van Laan, Nancy.
Moose tales / Nancy Van Laan ; illustrated by Amy Rusch.
p.   cm.
Summary: In three stories for beginning readers, Moose takes a walk,
takes a nap under a tree that Beaver is gnawing, and finally joins all
his friends in making an almost perfect snow creature with antlers.
ISBN 0-395-90863-9
[1. Moose—Fiction. 2. Animals—Fiction.] I. Rusch, Amy, ill.   II. Title.
PZ7.V3269Mo   1999
[E]—dc21   97-41273   CIP   AC

Manufactured in the United States of America
WOZ 10 9 8 7 6 5 4 3 2 1

Contents

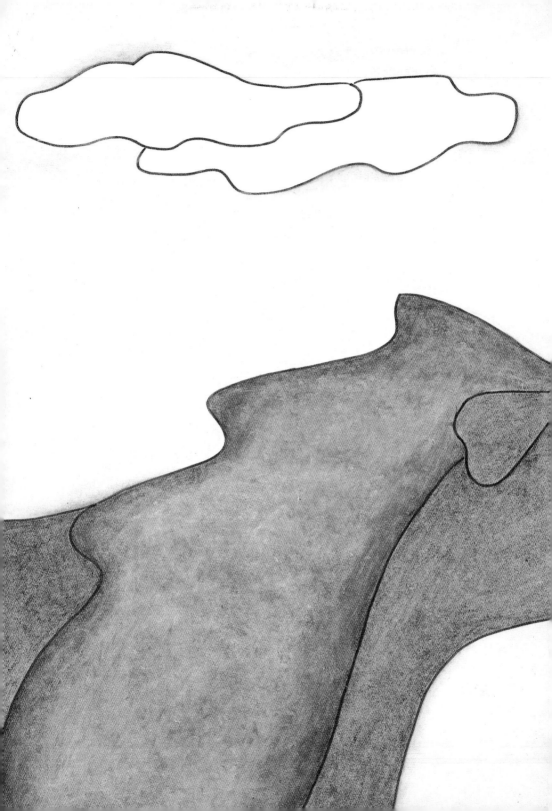

A Fine Day for a Walk

Moose sniffed the air.
It was a blue-sky day.
A sunshiny day.
A fine day for a walk.
Maybe Beaver would like to walk, too.

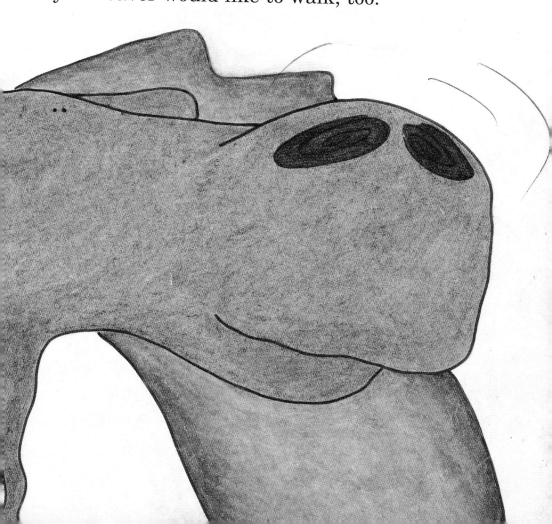

Moose walked up the hill and down the hill.

Moose walked to the pond to see Beaver.

"Hello, Beaver," said Moose. "It is a blue-sky day. A sunshiny day. A fine day for a walk."

"It is also a good day to swim," said Beaver.
"You are right," said Moose. "But my legs say it is time for a nice long walk."
"Ask Mouse," said Beaver. "Maybe Mouse will walk with you."
"Good idea," said Moose. "I will go ask Mouse."

Moose walked up the hill and down the hill.
Up and down another hill.

Moose walked across the meadow to see Mouse.

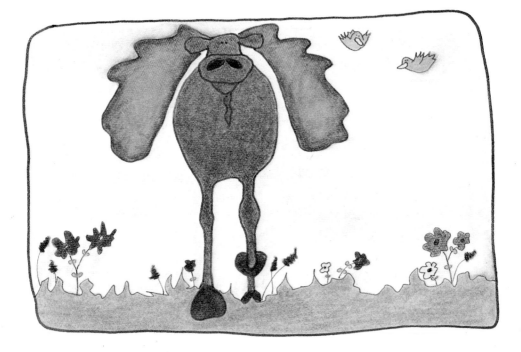

"Hello, Mouse," said Moose. "It is a blue-sky day.
A sunshiny day. A fine day for a walk."

"Yes," said Mouse. "It is also a good day to clean."
"You are right," said Moose. "But my legs say it is
time for a nice long walk."
"Ask Rabbit," said Mouse. "Maybe Rabbit will walk
with you."
"Good idea," said Moose. "I will go ask Rabbit."

Moose walked up the hill and down the hill.

Up the hill and down the hill.

Up and down another hill.

Moose walked across the corn field to see Rabbit.

"Hello, Rabbit," said Moose. "It is a blue-sky day. A sunshiny day. A fine day for a walk."

"Yes," said Rabbit. "It is also a good day to dig."
"You are right," said Moose. "But my legs say it is time for a nice long walk."
"Ask Squirrel," said Rabbit. "Maybe Squirrel will walk with you."
"Good idea," said Moose. "I will go ask Squirrel."

Moose walked up the hill and down the hill.

Up the hill. Down the hill.

Up. Down. Up and down another hill.

Moose walked through the woods to see Squirrel.

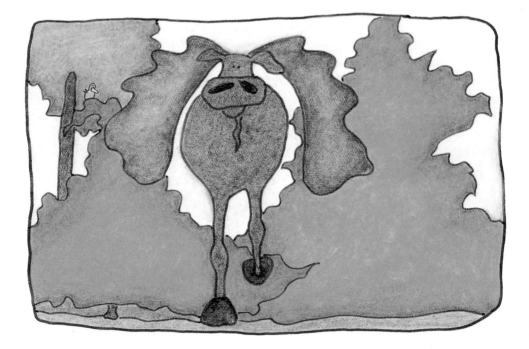

"Hello, Squirrel," said Moose. "It is a blue-sky day. A sunshiny day. A fine day for a walk."

"Yes," said Squirrel. "It is also a good day to climb."
"You are right," said Moose. "But my legs say it is time for a nice long walk."
"Ask Beaver," said Squirrel. "Maybe Beaver will walk with you."
"Hmmm..." said Moose. "Beaver has had time to swim. Maybe he is ready to walk now."

Moose walked up the hill and down the hill.

Up the hill. Down the hill.

Up. Down. Up. Down.

Moose walked back to the pond to see Beaver.

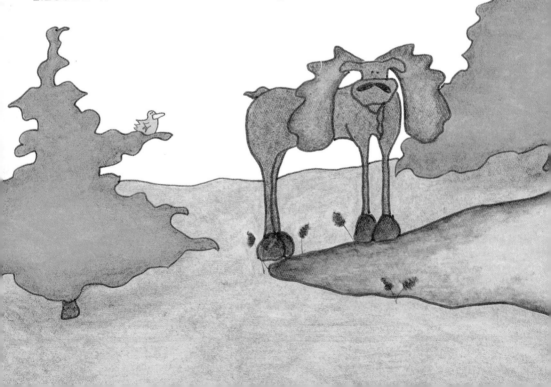

"Hello, Moose," said Beaver. "I am ready to go for a walk with you."

"Hmmm..." said Moose. "My legs are telling me something."
"What are they telling you?" asked Beaver.

"To take a nice long rest!" said Moose.
And that is just what Moose did.

Stuck

Beaver was busy.

He was busy gnawing a tall tree.

Moose was busy, too.

He was busy watching Beaver.

"Are you almost done?" asked Moose.

Beaver slung his tail sideways.

That meant no.

"Watching you work makes me sleepy," said Moose.
He lay down under the tree.
"I think I will take a nap."

The tree was very wobbly.
As Beaver gnawed, the tree wobbled back and forth.
Back and forth it went.
"Watch out, Moose," said Beaver.
Moose did not hear him. He was sound asleep.

"Wake up," said Beaver. "You are in the wrong spot."
"I am?" said Moose.

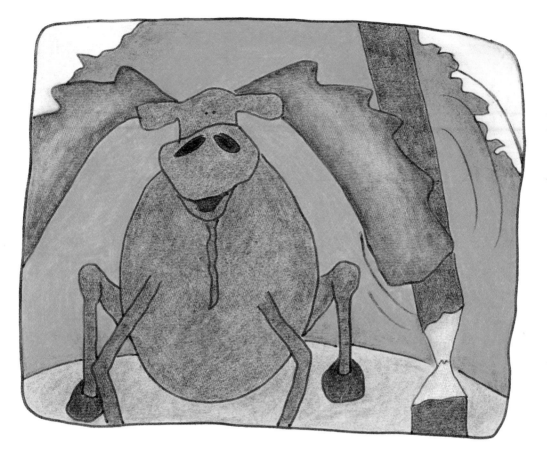

Moose stood up. He was not very awake.
His legs wobbled. Just like the tree.

Moose stumbled, then bumped into the tree—*hard!*
Down fell the tree! PLOP!
"Oh, no!" cried Beaver.
Moose turned around. Where was Beaver?
"Oh, dear me!" said Moose. "Are you all right?"

"I am fine," said Beaver. "Just stuck."

"Stay calm," said Moose. "I will sound my alarm."
Moose bellowed.
Everyone came at once.
"Beaver is stuck," said Moose. "We must
unstick him."
"How?" said Mouse and Rabbit and Squirrel.

"Gnaw the tree," said Beaver.

"Good idea!" said Moose.

Everyone gnawed. Even Moose.

But nobody had long sharp teeth like Beaver.

Gnawing was too hard to do.

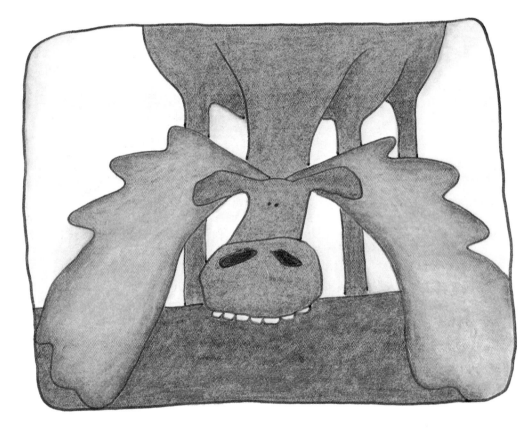

"I give up!" said Mouse.

"So do I!" said Squirrel.

"Oh, dear!" said Moose.

"Let's dig a hole," said Rabbit. "Then Beaver can crawl out."

"Good idea!" said Moose.

Everyone dug. Even Moose.

But a deep hole was too hard to dig.

"I give up!" said Mouse.

"So do I!" said Squirrel.

"Oh, dear!" said Moose.

"Maybe we should come back tomorrow," said Rabbit.

"Tomorrow!" cried Beaver. "Tomorrow is too long to be stuck!"

"It was my fault," said Moose. "I should be the one who is stuck."

"No," said Beaver. "You are too big. You would be stuck forever."

"Hmmm…" said Moose. "I am also very heavy."

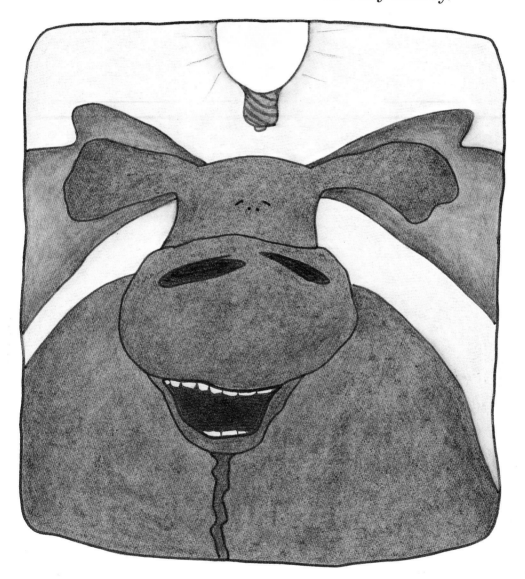

"Stand back, everybody!"

Moose sat down.
Up shot the other end of the tree!

Out ran Beaver. Beaver was unstuck!
"Hooray!" said Rabbit and Mouse and Squirrel.

The next day, Beaver went back to work.
He was busy gnawing a tree.
Moose was busy, too.
But Moose was not busy watching Beaver—
he was busy making a sign.
Moose put the sign near the tree.
It said: Do Not Nap Here.

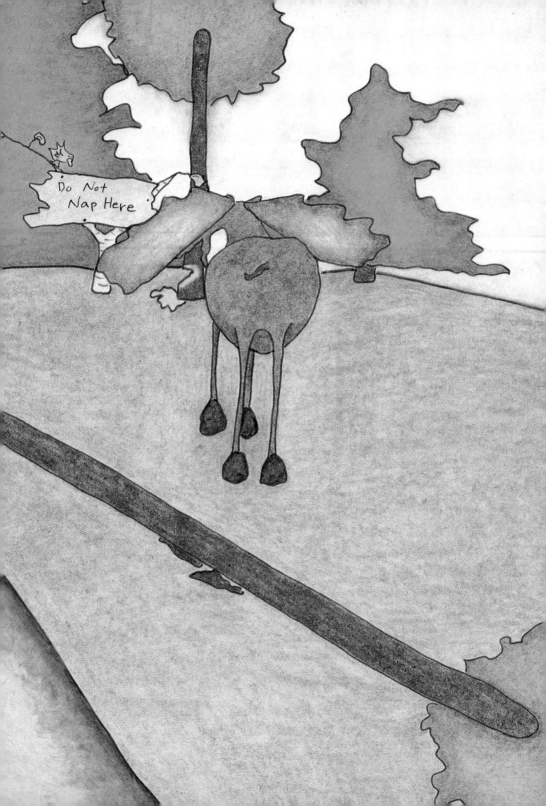

The Snow Creature

"It's snowing!" said Beaver.
"Hooray!" cried Moose.

Thick wet flakes tumbled from the sky.

"Let's catch them!" said Beaver.

"Let's count them!" said Moose.

Beaver and Moose lay down on the ground.

They looked up.

"One...two...three...four..." said Moose.

"Five hundred...seven thousand...one trillion..."
said Beaver.

"Too many to count," said Moose.

"Way too many," said Beaver.

Moose laughed. "Snow tickles!"

"It tickles my nose," said Beaver.

"It tickles my ears," said Moose.

"It tickles my eyelids," said Beaver.

"Open your mouth," said Moose.

"Now it tickles my tongue!" said Beaver.

"Let's be very still and see what happens,"
said Moose.
Beaver and Moose lay side by side.
Very still.
Soon they were under a blanket of soft snow.

Along came Mouse, Rabbit, and Squirrel.

Moose and Beaver sat up.

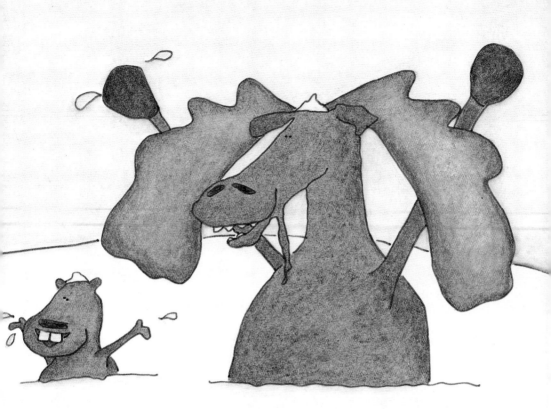

SURPRISE!

"Let's make a snow creature," said Moose.
Together they rolled and rolled a big ball of snow.

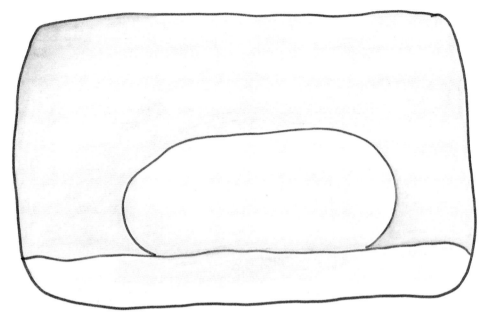

Next they rolled and rolled another ball.
It was smaller than the first.

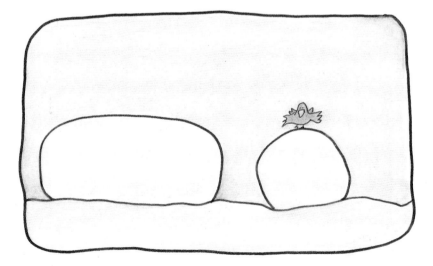

Together they placed the giant ball on top of four logs.

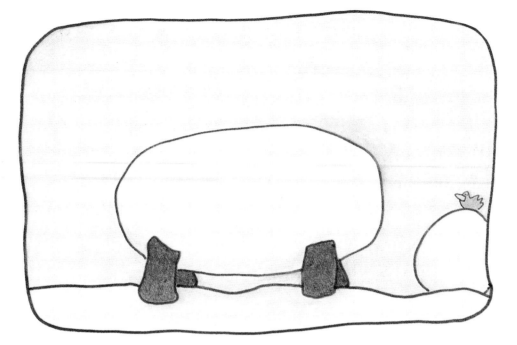

Next they attached the smaller ball.

"Hmmm…" said Moose. "Something is missing."

Beaver added two eyes and a nose.

"Something is still missing," said Moose.

"I know!" said Squirrel.

Squirrel added a long bushy tail.

"Hmmm…" said Moose. "Something is still missing."
"I know!" said Rabbit.
Rabbit added two long, thin ears.

"Hmmm…" said Moose. "Something is still missing."
"I know!" said Mouse.
Mouse added whiskers.

"Hmmm…" said Moose. "Something is still missing."

"I know!" said Beaver.

Beaver added two large teeth.

"Now it is all done!" said Mouse and Beaver and
Rabbit and Squirrel.

"No, it is not," said Moose.

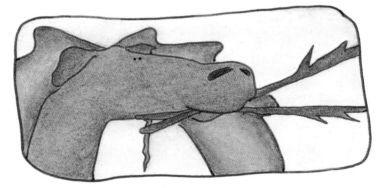

Moose placed a bare branch on each side of the
creature's head.

"Antlers," said Moose. "That is what was missing."

ogether they admired their creation.

. think it is practically perfect," said Moose.

Me, too," said Beaver.

Me, too," said Squirrel.

Me, too," said Rabbit.

Me, too," said Mouse.

And it was.